THE LAST SON OF
CHARYBDIS

Gabriel Anthony Lopez

iUniverse books may be ordered through booksellers or by contacting:

iUniverse
1663 Liberty Drive
Bloomington, IN 47403
www.iuniverse.com
844-349-9409

Because of the dynamic nature of the Internet, any web addresses or links contained in this book may have changed since publication and may no longer be valid. The views expressed in this work are solely those of the author and do not necessarily reflect the views of the publisher, and the publisher hereby disclaims any responsibility for them.

Any people depicted in stock imagery provided by Getty Images are models, and such images are being used for illustrative purposes only. Certain stock imagery © Getty Images.

ISBN: 978-1-6632-1285-6 (sc)
ISBN: 978-1-6632-1302-0 (e)

Library of Congress Control Number: 2020922142

Print information available on the last page.

iUniverse rev. date: 11/06/2020

In Memory
Cherri Ann Hurley Brinley

January 23, 1956 - August 30, 2008

Miss Cherri Ann Hurley Brinley inspired me in the realms of science. She especially inspired my imagination to write about science fiction. She also inspired me to aspire my dreams to educate myself throughout life. Science was her passion and the people in her life, which helped me further to connect me with my passion for everything science. Science and faith were at the heart of Miss Cherri Ann Hurley Brinley.

"…boot prints lay heavy around the tiny pool, the lush, well-tended green churned to mud. At one end of the garden, beneath a narrow out-crop, he had dug a shallow grave.

—*The Book of Atrus, Myst*

I

A trix wandered beside the pool. Byeolsu walked out of the pool. He was talking to Cephei.

"Who do you think won?" he said.

Cephei grabbed him and pinched his shoulders.

"I think it, it was left up to the trix," he laughed.

The both walked out of the pool and walked through the hypercenter and did not look behind as the door closed making everything around the two shimmer. The juxtaposed moon made the pool glisten and an eerie fog wisped around the pool. A shadow was seen at the other side.

Byeolsu made his way through the forest.

"So, how is Sirius?" he asked Cephei.

"Fine for the time being," he said, "He's out with the rest of the caste closing the rest of the hyper gates." He looked up at the night sky the stars twinkled back at him. The _trix_ started to squawk while sitting on a nearby rock as it looked up at a nearby shooting star.

"Oh," said Byeolsu. "The rest of the caste should be sleeping by now." He looked down at his wristband which began to glow and an image popped up on a nearby tree of his father Negral.

"Byeolsu, where are you?" he asked.

"I am at the nearby pool, father" said Byeolsu.

"Good, come back home, your mother and grandmother are waiting for you," he said with a dismissive smile. Byeolsu looked at Cephei and gave him a head nod. They both started to run in a sprint to get back to the nearest shadow and the both disappeared into the night as they touched their wristbands.

II

"I am star travelling together with you…"—Albrecht Dieterich

Zuma and Sia were seated at their rightful places around in the dining hall as Cephei and Byeolsu appeared out of the shimmer of firelight. As soon as Byeolsu materialized, Sia gave him a great big hug. "I'm so glad to see you, I was so worried about you," as she gave him the characteristic blessing on his forehead.

Zuma scowled at Byeolsu, but she still beckoned at him with her hand. Byeolsu looked over to Cephei and bowed. Cephei nodded.

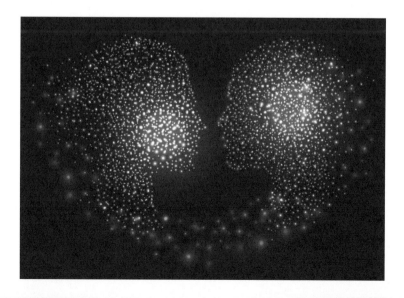

He touched his wristband and disappeared into the night contrasted by firelight. Zuma also gave the characteristic blessing.

"When was the last time you saw Errai," she said.

"It's been awhile" Byeolsu chuckled, "But, the last time I saw him, he ordered me to do three games in one of the major pools with Cephei."

"Where is Errai?" she inquired.

"He's in the other room," Zuma responded hesitantly.

Byeolsu walked into the adjacent room and saw Errai around a low table with a _xenozhu_ at his feet. A tapestry hanging behind Errai of ancient battles with _xenozhus_ calling home warriors from the fight moved back and forth against firelight in the clavet.

Errai glanced at Byeolsu.

"I see the wristbands are functioning properly. How many games did you go up against Cephei with this time?" he asked as he moved over from the table to let Byeolsu eat. Byeolsu touched the wristband and made sure he would not materialize naked in front of his grandfather. The xenozhu bayed in front of Byeolsu and gently pawed at him.

"Do you remember the first time you played bainet? But, then again you were young," Errai boosted to make sure Zuma and Sia may hear at the other end of the clavet.

"Yes, I do remember the first time I played grandfather. Cephei and I played both above the water and below and with hoverboards. Cephei said his wristband kept beeping as if something formidable was out there in the forest or around the mountains, but it was only a trix running around the pool," Byeolsu said, as he patted the xenozhu.

Errai pointed behind him at the tapestry as he ate more and ordered one of the slave women nearby him to get more food.

"Do you remember the story of the first game started from one of the pools. The one called Toani." Errai clasped his hands together as Byeolsu ate. "The first game," Errai said, "was supposedly started by the ancestor-god Ipal. The hieroglyphics around the pool explain the game's story further. Maybe you can make it there one day."

"I see," said Byeolsu "There were hieroglyphics around this pool. But I was too busy trying to beat Cephei to decern them. He was winning 1-0 with the ball behind his line. The trix kept squawking so I knew the sun had gone down and the moon was up and the hypercenter was coming online."

Errai finally finished what the slave gave him to eat and motioned at the side of the calvet in a gesture with his hand.

"Why don't you spend the night here before we move across Charybdis again," he said sleepily, clapping his hands together for the rest of the slaves to clean off the table.

"Sure," Byeolsu said, "I'll spend the night here and go back to one pool to play against Cephei."

Byeolsu quickly got up from the table and made sure not to disturb the xenozhu slumbering and made his way to the other side of the clavet and touched his wristband to turn off the two orbs of light surrounding his bed—used to read a book at night with or for protection—and gently put himself inside the covers of the bed. He sang an ancient hymn only sung at the end of a game and he only heard the caw of a trix again in the night surrounding him.

III

"…I find myself in a psychically unfree state of possession…"—Carl Jung

Byeolsu woke up to the binary sun's rays splintering across the room. On the other side, Errai was sleeping. His wristband was beeping. He touched it.

"Byeolsu, may the gods bless you this morning," said Cephei.

"Same," said Byeolsu under hush brush and still under the elixir of sleep.

"How was your sleep?" beckoned Cephei as his form came together to Byeolsu over the wristband.

"It was fine, it was fine," said Byeolsu. "Are we going to Orleans, the capital, or are we staying at the same pool?"

Cephei looked uncomfortable.

"What's wrong?" said Byeolsu.

"We will wait until later today to go the capital. We will be at the pool playing bainet today before we discern some hieroglyphics there," said Cephei.

Byeolsu got and put on some new clothes and wore his headband and adjusted his wristband. Errai snored in the distance as he grabbed his hoverboard and took flight down a hallway of the calvet. Byeolsu thought of his mother and grandmother and what would become of today's game. The hypercenter was open and he entered into the shimmering light.

"Scat!" said Cephei as Byeolsu emerged from the to a trix. A *taqueti* was licking a puddle of ide beside the pool as binary light rays bounced across the forest. Byeolsu took the hoverboard to the middle of the pool. Cephei too took to the middle of the pool and bounced a ball and turned on his headband.

Cephei let a grunt and said, "This one is for discerning hieroglyphics today!" And, his head lit up and the ball was thrown to Byeolsu. Byeolsu's headband lit up as well and he blocked the maneuver as the headband absorbed more rays from the sun and heat from his body. Byeolsu returned the favor by gaining a point from Cephei as the ball crossed the goal.

"Do you know where you're from Byeolsu and what you're from?" said Cephei

"What do you mean? I always thought I was from this area next to the capital of Orleans" Byeolsu chided.

He gained the ball. "Point!" Byeolsu said. Waves of the pool lapped against the side of the forest. The commotion scared a *taqueti* and it ran into the forest. Byeolsu slammed the ball against the water of the pool and it quickly caught Cephei off guard and went straight into the pool.

"Better luck next time!" said Byeolsu to Cephei.

"You have a thing or two to learn Byeolsu about the game and today" said Cephei.

"And please god, don't roll your eyes at me Byeolsu" Cephei reprimanded.

Instead, Byeolsu did.

"That was a good game and maneuver Byeolsu. But, today, we have something even more to learn. Today, we learn about where you're from," said Cephei.

"And by that your meaning…" said Byeolsu.

"Don't ruin the story. It isn't just a story, a fact," said Cephei. "You're almost over the age to play bainet."

"Well that's no good that I'm over the age to play bainet and I'm to learn a fact today," said Byeolsu.

Cephei nodded and turned his hoverboard over to the cliff where a small waterfall cascading down into the pool. Byeolsu looked on hesitantly. He summoned up the courage as he tapped the hoverboard and made his way to the cliff. When Byeolsu arrived by Cephei, Cephei started to point in gladness.

"This is your grandfather's grandfather need I say more," Cephei eyes glistening and popped a piece chua in his mouth.

"Well, I see, but what is the big deal," said Byeolsu.

Cephei answered, "This one glyph says that your grandmother's husband, your grandfather on your mother's side, is from the Imperium which makes you the last son of Charybdis. I'm just a Charybdisian a son of some slaves."

"What does that mean? How does that separate me from you and Sirius? I've only known you two for most of my life," Byeolsu gulped.

"We will find out today by going to market at the imperial capital of Orleans. Grab your hoverboard and let's go!" said Cephei. Cephei took the hoverboard and tapped the back of it and zoomed off over the waterfall. Byeolsu followed.

IV

"He might drown; he thinks of the assault of enemies, of wild animals, and can't get away. He is in an utterly exposed situation. He has to realize he can't move away he can't escape the onslaught of unconsciousness, and he needs protection badly."

—C.G. Jung, *Dream of Symbols of the Individuation Process*

The market hummed and bustled as usual to Cephei under the Imperial towers. Cephei walked over to shadowy side of the market looking for Sirius and found him. They both bowed and shook their hands.

"Did Byeolsu hear of the story that is now a fact," he said to Cephei.

"Yes, he did. He'll get over his new life." Cephei said. "He has not heard the full story but he will such as the one where I am technically held by the mother's side of the family as a son of slaves and not the last son of Charybdis the future ruler of this planet," Cephei added.

Sirius touched the corner of his eye and wiped away a tear, "Oh," he said to Cephei. "Not many admit to that these days Cephei about who rule Charybdis and where we are all from on this almost dying world. In the market, I keep hearing the mines are going and the food is getting bad," he added.

"Well Byeolsu will learn his lesson today about who his friends are and his enemies. Both you and I know we can no longer protect from the secret of the political situation on Charybdis and what his family is and who he is related to in the Imperium," said Cephei.

"Isn't it obvious?" Sirius moaned. "He's the last ruler of this planet."

"I think he played too much bainet on the pools when he was growing," said Cephei.

Byeolsu quickly flew past both Sirius and Cephei and grabbed a piece of chua from one of the marketers and flipped him a coin. He jumped off the hoverboard and quickly started to make his way through the crowd. It was a cloudy day, and one of the suns showed through the clouds. Someone bumped shoulders with him and laughed. Byeolsu touched his hand and blood started to run down his fingers.

"O my god!" he said out loud. No one heard him. He looked behind him. All that was left was a shadowy wisp of air against the shine of merchandise from the market against the sunlight. Byeolsu quickly ran to the nearest medpod bay stationed across the market. He touched it with his wristband. Quickly the medpod bay lowered itself and Byeolsu grabbed some bandages and a hypospray. He injected himself quickly and administered the bandages on his upper arm and wiped the blood from his fingers with a cloth.

Both Sirius and Cephei were nowhere to be seen. The medpod bay for some reason quickly shut off. Byeolsu wondered why the medpod bay was not working. A robot appeared out of the corner of Byeolsu's eye. "May I assist you, sir" chimed the robot.

"No, I'm fine, just fine!" barked Byeolsu. He needed to find a way to hide the wound from Sirius and Cephei.

"Where is the nearest medpod bay, robot!" exclaimed Byeolsu.

"The nearest medpod bay is in section A3 of the market. Please take your hoverboard. It will be about 3.8 COUs from this medpod bay," said the robot. Byeolsu grabbed his hoverboard and jumped on it and began swerving through the street of the market. Byeolsu thought to himself "I hope Sirius and Cephei don't find me. They are starting to give up their protection like most Charybdisians these days are in light of the recent political developments." With all the swerving, Byeolsu finally made it to the medpod bay and began administering everything to his wound and body.

Byeolsu made his way over to Sirius and Cephei.

"Ha-ha, my brother! How has your day been?" said Sirius and Cephei as quirky as ever the two of them are together commented Byeolsu. Did they not notice the bulge from the bandage on his right arm? he thought.

"It's been alright I bought some *chua* when I first hoverboarded in and since been just making my way around the market to you two," quipped Byeolsu.

"Why such the disgruntled look on your face?" said Sirius.

"Well for one thing" said Byeolsu, "It's getting kind of hot underneath the suns. A game of bainet you two?"

"Should we tell him again?" said Sirius to Cephei.

"Yes, we should" said Cephei, "But this time with the story of his mother. And, then the story meeting fact about us two and most Charybdisians."

"I would rather walk on the nearest *corcova*—or beach in another words—" said Byeolsu. "Maybe there will be a pool there."

Cephei and Sirius both bowed and took their hoverboards and programmed the hypercenter, the one beyond the Imperial towers and market. Byeolsu was behind them when Sirius touched his wristband to the hypercenter. As all three of them walked through the hypercenter and shimmered along with it, a fourth figure appeared behind Byeolsu causing a fire where the wristbands touch the hypercenter.

V

The mind is a terrible thing to waste—Unknown

All three emerged onto the *corcova* and with them the shadowy figure. Byeolsu ran through the sand like a child again as Cephei and Sirius both laughed. Byeolsu touched his wristband to accelerate the process of healing his arm. The waves of the ocean lapsed against the sand. Byeolsu retired to the nearest hieroglyphic pool while Sirius and Cephei ate lunch together on a fossilized log tossed by the waves for centuries.

Byeolsu started to bounce one of the bainet balls on the water, but for some reason light caught Byeolsu's eyes where the hieroglyphics were located and his pupils dilated. Every time he bounced the ball the hieroglyphics glowed and dazzled and then faded. Enticed Byeolsu went over to the hieroglyphs to inspect. He tried to touched one of the ancient hieroglyphs and dots of what seemed like red diamonds poured from the inscription.

Byeolsu took this as an omen. He heard Cephei and Sirius playing bainet in the background and stepped onto his hoverboard to join them.

"Find anything intriguing," said Sirius.

"Well, yes," said Byeolsu as all three bounced their ball against the water.

The oceanic waves crashed against the rocks and cliffs separating the almost sacred bainet pool from the rest of the tumultuous water of Charybdis. The game ended 2 Byeolsu 3 Sirius and 1 Cephei. It was twilight when Sirius began to notice a dark figure approaching them in the distant the light of the binary stars was of no help. "Who is that he wondered?"

Both Byeolsu and Cephei were sleeping in the far-off distance when Sirius decided to go down to the corcova to protect both Byeolsu and Cephei from the ominous figure.

"Who are you?" shouted Sirius.

As Sirius is from the slave mining families form Charybdis, Byeolsu was more trained at bainet and the power of the headband. He adjusted it to the position of the sun. His body warmed and his left and right hand both glowed in the twilight.

The shadowy figure laughed and snarled at what Sirius just did. To Sirius' well-trained eye, a humanoid emerged from shadowy, darkness. The humanoid was a man and did not look like any Charybdisian he knew. Finally, the humanoid took proper form. The man had a square jaw with a scar crossing his face from one eye to the next.

The man spat on the *corcova* and said, "I am Enceladus, and who are you not to notice these times of insurrection."

"Insurrection from whom," said Sirius.

"Well, you know the one you are protecting, the young one named Byeolsu," said Enceladus with a handclap.

"What do you want with him?" said Sirius.

"Well, I want him dead for one thing" said Enceladus.

Sirius powered up his head band until his hands not only glowed with the power of the two binary stars but in the middle blue light showed through the twilight the power of fire was finally harnessed by Sirius.

In midst of fury, at Enceladus's answer, Sirius threw the blazing light from his hands at Enceladus as his headband glowed even further—a sign of impending doom. Enceladus blocked the power Sirius was emitting with his hand and threw it back at him. Murdering Sirius in the twilight with nothing of him remaining, but footprints leading up to the scene of the fight. A trix cawed at the moon rising and the two binary stars twinkled out of view of Enceladus.

VI

"War is to feel like the sun to them." —*The Book of Tournaments, Charybdis II*

Byeolsu's eyes opened to the dark sky and to Cephei snoring. Byeolsu was not fully awake as he just realized the saliva of a _taqueti_ was on his face. It was still running away in the distance. Byeolsu moved Cephei.

"Psst," said Byeolsu, "Where is Sirius?"

"I don't know," said Cephei, "Let's go back to the calvet."

Byeolsu took a quick look around the beach—or corcova in his family's language—and noticed a strange sight in the sky. It was metallic and a halo of orange light emitted from its ventral sides. What is it he wondered?

Cephei put both of his hands on Byeolsu's shoulder's, "Something happened Byeolsu. The Imperium would not have released the much ore to build a floating fortress in some time."

"What does it mean?" Byeolsu inquired.

"I have no idea," said Cephei.

Cephei put his shirt back on and Byeolsu did likewise. They both garnered enough bodily energy to get back on their hoverboards and program them to the ancient pool back where Byeolsu's family calvet is with Zuma, Sia, and Errai.

Byeolsu and Cephei zoomed up over the _corcova_ and went into the forest. A heard of dukeis ran alongside them for the majority of the run to the calvet. As they neared the ancient pool and forest, Byeolsu prayed that everyone was alright. Byeolsu and Cephei entered the other side of the calvet away from the ancient pool and forest. Everyone was sleeping.

"Where is Sirius?" Byeolsu inquired. "He's not here."

Cephei shrugged his shoulders as the son of the slaves who are serving the finally family to rule Charybdis he could care less about the son of some miners.

Byeolsu glared at him.

"Time to hit the orbs," and Cephei did so. And, Cephei immediately did so and lit up a feathered bed from a small _taqueti_. Byeolsu growled.

"I just think something is wrong," he said.

"Stop worrying you said like Sia and Zuma," said Cephei.

Byeolsu jumped inside his bed and touched his wristband to turn off the orbs of light surrounding him.

"Until tomorrow," said Cephei.

Cephei woke up Byeolsu to go to the market. When they both arrived, the Imperial Towers of Orleans shined brightly in the dawn. Cephei nodded to Byeolsu in concurrence with what he said earlier that *something had happened.* Cephei decided to guard the gate of the market and Orleans while Byeolsu scouted inside the capital. A robot inquired about Byeolsu's entrance into the capital and market.

"What are you doing here? Do you not know what is going on?" said the robot, its metalloid features glistening in the daylight after the dawn.

"What do you mean?" said Byeolsu.

"I believe an insurrection has started of the Imperium, their looking for its ruler and the family that he is from on Charybdis. Even the mines are rioting and insurrecting and the Imperium is finally releasing spaceships to stop the insurrection," said the robot in a stilted voice. Suddenly, Byeolsu saw not one, but three robots all attempting to surround him.

Byeolsu touched his wristband, but was not prepared to use the power of his headband. However, it started to glow with the warmth of his body and the light of the binary stars.

He looked to the left of him and saw a chance to hop over the ancient marble walls of Orleans. He did not want to touch and fight a group of robots now who were insurrecting because of the loss of power to the Imperium and release of spaceships. So, he chose to climb over the marble walls while touching his wristband to increase the size of his jump.

Byeolsu spoke into his wristband to give Cephei a message to stay away from the market and the Imperial Towers. Byeolsu looked up and saw two spaceships hovering over the capital of Orleans. More robots descended from a beam emitted by the spaceships. As Byeolsu, started to run; he heard screaming from the city. He did not want to look back at the slaughter he thought would start. From the time him, Sirius, and Cephei were at the corcova and this morning Charybdis had been insurrecting according to the robot.

Byeolsu was alone finally. He placed the hoverboard at his side while he started to weep. He did not know where Cephei or Sirius were and it frightened him. Byeolsu could not believe he chose to run from a fight despite his bainet training all these years. A group of _dukeis_ wandered aimlessly from grassy knoll to grassy knoll. Byeolsu kicked his hoverboard. Fury ran down his face and Byeolsu clenched his fists. Who were they after? Cephei told him a secret that he was the future ruler of Charybdis, but he did not believe him. He convinced himself he must talk to his father, Negral, at the Imperial Council on the western side of the city.

VII

If there is a will then there's a way—Unknown

Byeolsu walked upon the blue marble steps of the Imperial Council on the western side of the city of Orleans. He must talk to his father, Negral. Byeolsu moved his way into the hallway of the Imperial Council. Byeolsu did not know who they were after; all he knew was his father *sat* on the Imperial Council. To the best of Byeolsu's knowledge he was no one of importance nor was his father, Negral.

Byeolsu remembers Cephei's words, but that is coming from the son of slaves. He could not believe he lived among Sirius and Cephei. All to suit his mother, Sia, and his grandmother Zuma. Byeolsu finally entered the Council Chamber, and he saw his father on a podium amid the empty room.

Byeolsu ran to him. And, when he finally got up to the top of the podium, he finally realizes the stoicism of his father. "Byeolsu, what are you doing here?" said Negral. Negral wristband was plugged into the library of the Imperial Council lightening up his headband as well.

"Father," he said, "I came to rescue you. I saw spaceships above the capital, and robots coming down in a beam."

"Very well," said Negral.

He tapped the wristband to shut down and the headband around him stopped glowing.

"Have you spoken to mother, grandmother and grandfather?" said Byeolsu.

"Yes, I have," said Negral.

"Are they safe?" said Byeolsu.

"Yes, they are safe," Negral reaffirmed. "In fact,", he said, "they are now evacuating Charybdis to Charybdis II."

Byeolsu nodded. He knew he had much to learn but did not know they had another planet named after the current one. It is probably terraformed. The political seeds of destruction were sowed on Charybdis, but Byeolsu still did not know why nor his father.

Byeolsu motioned to his father to clasp both their wristbands together and teleport back to the calvet to save the last remnants of Charybdis I. The Imperial Council room after Negral and Byeolsu teleported back to the calvet was then abruptly taken by insurrectionists. A band of robots stood outside forever banning the once and future ruler of Charybdis. More spaceships arrived and a beam from one of them came down on the marble steps before the robots. A shadowy, humanoid figure began to appear and quickly ran up to one of the robots. It was Enceladus.

He had a wristband on—possibly Sirius's—and hijacked the program of one of the robots. He grabbed the head of one of the robots and screamed. He had one message to give as he linked up with the robot to all remaining Charybdisians. Leave or die.

VIII

And, you call yourself a Christian—Unknown

Byeolsu boarded a rogue spaceship loyal to the Imperium and his family. Charybdis II is the destination. Byeolsu looked around the ship. Zuma, Sia, and Errai were being carried shoulder to shoulder to another part of the ship down a steep incline on the ship. Byeolsu looked at the viewscreen. More and more spaceships loyal to the insurrection were coming upon the capital of Orleans. The two binary stars pulsated in the distance and the dark side of Charybdis I was giving off light from populated areas.

A Captain approached Byeolsu saying more squadrons of the fleet are coming to help out any remaining Charybdisians who wanted to flee the planet.

Byeolsu agreed to enter a hyper sleep chamber in preparation for the journey to Charybdis II. Before Byeolsu entered into the hyper sleep chamber he kept his headband and touched his wristband to the hyper sleep chamber and watched the final bainet game with Cephei and Sirius—still wondering what happened to Sirius and Cephei. Did Cephei stay on the planet or board one of the ships? Did Sirius get taken hostage? There were so many questions as Byeolsu fell asleep.

Many of the Charybdisians fell asleep in their hyper sleep chambers all alone in the night of space. The fleet wandered aimlessly for about four months in deep space and finally arrived at Charybdis II, a terraformed planet. Its sole purpose to save the Imperium and the family ruling it from certain destruction and Charybdisians along with it. It had two moons and a vast ocean. Covered with green and lakes it did not emulate the almost desert of Charybdis I and the constant mining occurring on the planet and its moon.

Byeolsu wristband woke him up beneath the containment field of the sleep chamber. He rubbed his eyes. Awake again many Charybdisians were already and going to the nearest dispenser of food. Byeolsu knew that his family was safe for the time being, but still did not know where Sirius was and Cephei. A dream, came to him when he was asleep in the hyper chamber. It was a dream of the mind-benders that were originally on Charybdis I that he failed to encounter after meeting the robots amid the insurrection that started of Charybdis I. As he put his clothes back on, he gradually realized he had much work to do on Charybdis II. A capital did exist on Charybdis II called Orgoz but had laid abandoned since almost beyond the time of his grandfather.

Byeolsu made his way to the chair of a Captain and asked him to teleport him down to the surface. With his wristband and headband on, it was done. Orgoz was abandoned. The opulence of the capital was no more as the surrounding forest and vegetation gradually reclaimed what was theirs. A group of trix wandered through a hallway Byeolsu was wandering through to get to the main chamber to insert his wristband in the library.

On the other side of the chamber, was a massive group of tablets with modern hieroglyphics on them— the writing of Charybdis II. Byeolsu began to study them. He brought out a glass piece emulating ancient microscope technology and was wowed at the complexity of the new language thought by his forefathers. None of these words led to the key that Cephei and Sirius were alluding too. Suddenly, Byeolsu heard a noise and a scream. It was a fellow Charybdisian from the original planet. There was a new insurrection he feared that of something fowl which is only comes about when hyper sleep chambers are used. The mind-benders were at work, and were about to work on Byeolsu, but not without a fight.

IX

Byeolsu walked out of the reading chamber and ran down a hallway to the outside of the Charybdis II's capital's main chamber room. It was situated on a plateau. A group of mind-benders were seen attempting to torture and remove the tattoos of ordinary Charybdisians. Most of Charybdis I's population held the tattoos with pride. The ink used was powerful. It was never mocked even though most knew it was attempt to emulate the ruling caste system called the Imperium and continued search for the once and future ruler of Charybdis.

Byeolsu was ready for a fight. A group of humanoids approached him. His headband lit up from the warmth of his body and the power of Charybdis II's single sun. Byeolsu decided to touch his wrist band and increase the power he was about to emit from his hands. He was not going to let the mind-benders anywhere near him. They had tortured a group of Charybdians and extracted their tattoos enslaving them in their minds. They humanoids were not maimed in any way from countless fighting as Charybdis I one was evacuating and spaceships flooding the cities of Charybdis I and further enslaving the population. Unfortunately, the mind-benders had more sophisticated headband technology and mind-altering substances to use on Byeolsu.

"Who are you?" screamed Byeolsu.

"Well you of all people should know Byeolsu once we get inside your mind this game of bainet is over with Enceladus," said the mind-bender lighting up his hand without touching his wristband and his headband glowed in the high noon light still. Byeolsu was quickly knocked off his feet by one of the mind-benders and in return Byeolsu created a shield of energy around him. And, got up barley scathed by the power to harness solar energy.

"Too late to create to a shield," said another mind-bender. The mind-benders originated from the desert on Charybdis I, but still possessed the tattoo. This mind-bender's tattoo started to glow and lightly touched it. Byeolsu had a small tattoo designating he was from the Imperium and his father Negral, and mother Sia. Three more of the mind-benders agreed with the gift and curse they all were about to give Byeolsu. The gift of knowing who he truly was.

All three mind-benders powered up their headbands and wristbands and automatically threw the solar energy at Byeolsu causing Byeolsu to bleed from the chest. As that happened, Byeolsu's headband and wrist band lit up recalibrating the damage done to his body to start the healing process. Byeolsu automatically touched his wristband to send a message to the rogue ship, Cephei, and Sirius. Byeolsu curled up in unbelievable pain, but somehow created a solar shield to absorb the energy of what was left of the mind-benders attack. He screamed in pain. His headband was definitely damaged. During the fight a message was received from the mind-benders.

"Are you the last ruler of Charybdis," the message said. "I think you are," it sounded off with the voice of mind-bender blaring through his brain.

Byeolsu kept the solar shield on well into the twilight and only came too once he was certain the mind-benders were no longer there. Looking for an answer to the blood and the damage done to his headband, Byeolsu needed some king of spiritual renewal. The fight zapped him of his energy and almost destroyed his headband. Byeolsu looked at his wristband and a message were received from on the Captains aboard the leading rogue ship carrying his family. He thought of his grandmother Zuma and the prophesy of the humanoids and what could be happening on Charybdis I.

X

"…Five of them were foolish and five were wise. The foolish ones when taking their lamps brought no oil with but the wise brought flasks of oil with their lamps…"

—Matthew 25: 2-3

Byeolsu ran through Orgoz's, the capital of Charybdis II, main capital chamber still bleeding from his side. Byeolsu said a prayer. He pressed his wristband up against his forehead to the tattoo to increase the solar energy already harnessed. His wristband beeped. Cephei was showed up on the wall next to him as a hologram.

"Where are you?" he said. "I evacuated with another ship. And, where is Sirius?"

Byeolsu responded, "I think I know. I think something happened to him on Charybdis I. I've been attacked by mind-benders from the desert of Charybdis I. We must find what happened to Sirius." Byeolsu thought he had enough energy to reach the spaceship he was on with his family and possibly Cephei's. But suddenly he was thrown up against the wall, the same wall which Cephei appeared as a hologram on which suddenly switched off in the twilight. Byeolsu screamed in pain.

"Look what you have done ruler of Charybdis," said a hoarse voice in his ear.

Byeolsu was handing upside down, but he managed to do a maneuver with his body taught by Sirius and Cephei. The humanoid did not release his grip immediately, but Byeolsu—killed him with the maneuver—Byeolsu's first. He remembered not to gloat if he ever used his bainet training. Byeolsu looked down at the body. It was a Charybdisian who was under the control of mind-altering substances during a fight with the mind-benders. He knew a Charybdisian would never attack a supposed ruler of Charybdis. All Byeolsu wanted to do was run and run vast away from the chambers and library of Orgoz. Byeolsu touched the eyes of the Charybdisian and closed them.

Byeolsu finally made his way out of chambers and held up his hand blocking the moonlight from his already tired eyes. He was looking for the rogue spaceships in the distance and found one glistening against the dark sky of Charybdis II shown by the new constellations of stars of the quadrant of space he was in from the evacuation. He checked the position of the constellations on a map on his wristband.

All was ripe for a spiritual renewal like his grandmother, Zuma, said. The defeat by the mind-benders did it, but it was only a victory said the prophesy of his family. He now knew who he was and that he was the one the insurrectionists were looking for on Charybdis I and what happened to Sirius. There was someone there waiting for him he just knew it. In front of him lay forest and hills and in the distance a snowy mountain range. He must make it to the spaceship carrying his family and make it back to Charybdis I. He must find what happened to Sirius. Byeolsu looked around him and he found a lonely xanadu to ride. Byeolsu went to it and grabbed it by its harness and kicked it on its side and touched the skin of the xanadu with his wristband. The xanadu belched and bayed and Byeolsu rode off into the distance to the rogue spaceships gathered in a line on the horizon.

XI

"There is only sadness."—The Book of Tournaments, Charybdis I

When Byeolsu entered into the spaceship, a worried group of evacuees began to pat his head, removing some of the crusty blood from his forehead. Byeolsu shook them off and admitted to them he had been in fight attempting to enslave them even further. He made his way through the corridors of the ship to the Captain at the front of the ship.

"Let's leave," ordered Byeolsu.

Byeolsu knew somehow the Captain knew of his secret to rule over Charybdis I once they meandered through deep space at light speed.

"It will take some time to get the hyper sleep chambers ready," said the Captain.

Byeolsu looked for his family and found out they were still sleeping in their hyper sleep chambers and Byeolsu had realized he had only been gone a day. Cephei entered behind him from a door adjacent to him.

"Byeolsu, my brother! How goes it?" he was not even stammering after evacuating and emerging from the hyper sleep chamber. Strong he is thought Byeolsu, but he was not strong enough to find Sirius which he resented.

"It goes fine," said Byeolsu. Did Cephei not know he got in fight with some mind-benders and was told the secret against Cephei's word and the prophesy of his grandmother Zuma and the ancient hieroglyphic was coming true. Byeolsu kept wandering about pools by the calvet still hopefully unscathed from insurrection on Charybdis I. Byeolsu knew something was tremendously out of place in the great scheme of prophetic principles once uttered by the Imperium on Charybdis I. Cephei clasped his hands together in hope Byeolsu was not suddenly become aware of who he truly is, but the effort of smiling and congratulating Byeolsu seemed almost futile in retrospect to Cephei.

"Are you ready for the long nap?" said Cephei.

"Yes, I am," murmured Byeolsu under conceited breath. Byeolsu touched his wristband and found the location of his hyper sleep chamber.

"Let's sleep beside one another just like the days of old, brother, when we played those games of bainet," he said while he too tapped his wristband and found the location of his hyper sleep chamber. Cephei alerted one of the evacuees to assist him in to get into the hyper sleep chamber. He too was seen by Byeolsu starting to hide the wear placed upon him by the deep slumber and the light speed effect often seen on Charybdisians after long distance travel. Byeolsu started to get paranoid fearing that he would lose his secret once he fell asleep. He touched his wristband to his headband. He screamed instead. It was there alright. The memory of the fight with the mind-benders and the message of his right to rule Charybdis I.

Byeolsu placed himself on the bed and straightened himself in place before the containment field went on around him. Byeolsu was worried about the prophesies seen around the calvet, the home of his family, and prophesy of humans approaching Charybdis I from the words of his grandmother. Insurrection had most definitely started on Charybdis I. A cadet began to walk through the aisles of sleep chambers and found Byeolsu's. She inputted some information on a tablet. The Captain called the cadet back to the front of the spaceship. As the cadet approached, the Captain inputted the code to achieve light speed. None of the evacuee ships would be alone in the dark of space for about a day.

XII

"As they beat him, they asked where he got the painting from. The country friend told them everything. They therefore brought both friends to the palace. The king said, 'You both have stolen the place's money so we can't let you live.' "

—A Korean Story, *A Painting That Will Make Your Wishes Come True*

When the armada of evacuee ships approached, Charybdis I the capital was beginning to take hits from insurrectionist spaceships as they continued to open fire. Byeolsu and his family after awaking from hyper sleep teleported back to the calvet. Standing next to them, all of them looked bewildered and shocked at the fate of Charybdis I. Byeolsu collected himself as Cephei teleported beside him. As soon as everyone came too and teleportation finished the materialization process, a robot smashed through the calvet. Cephei smashed his hand straight through the chest of the robot ending its robotic existence. Byeolsu collected himself again. Despite witnessing Cephei's anger, he was determined to know what happened to Sirius. Byeolsu motioned to Cephei.

"Let's go down to the corcova," he said without gasping a breath to Cephei.

Cephei remained unharmed during the fight with the robot and winked at Byeolsu.

Both Byeolsu and Cephei looked around the calvet and found their hoverboards. They both tapped their hoverboards on their sides and they quickly left to the corcova. As they passed through the thick forest full of less wildlife, Byeolsu checked to see if no harm was done to the ancient pool, he once played bainet on with Cephei and no harm as to the hieroglyphics by the pool was done.

Byeolsu and Cephei finally made it to the cliff which overlooked the ocean where he once slept after the loss of Sirius. Cephei went down from the cliff to check the condition of the hieroglyphics prophesying Byeolsu and the insurrection. Byeolsu instead went to the corcova—or beach—and began investigating a scene where some footprints were found. He determined that they were Sirius'. Byeolsu cried and as soon as he did a dark, shadowy humanoid figure appeared out of the corner of his eye.

"Well, congratulations, you found the murder of your life," said the figure.

"Who are you?" said Byeolsu.

"Well, would you stop wondering about your friend so quickly," said the humanoid.

"Shut up!" said Byeolsu.

"My name is Enceladus" he chimed. Byeolsu could see a scar from one eye to the other that marked his face.

"What did you do with Sirius" exclaimed Byeolsu.

"I killed him like all insurrectionists," said Enceladus.

"You are who and what again?!" screamed Byeolsu.

"An insurrectionist. Now, that I am. So, quit you're screaming and join the ranks of the dead," Enceladus. And, in one blazing move Enceladus powered up his headband and wristband and threw a huge bulge of solar energy at Byeolsu. Byeolsu blocked the move quickly having a solar shield absorb all the energy from

Enceladus. Cephei noticing the fight and came quickly by hoverboard. He stood beside a kneeling Byeolsu who was recalibrating his wristband and his headband which both glowed in the morning light.

Cephei charged up his wrist band and held a beam of the binary stars' light. He threw the beams at Enceladus but Enceladus still blocked them. The waves continued to crash against the rocks and the cliffs surrounding the three.

"Now, future, son of Charybdis and the last one at that. What are you going to do if you defeat me in this fight and battle on Charybdis I?" said Enceladus in a dismissive tone.

Byeolsu glared at him. The secret of the mind-benders on Charybdis II proved itself correct. He was the one the insurrectionists were after and the one the ancient hieroglyphics prophesied and so did his grandmother, Zuma. Byeolsu worried about his family he left back at the calvet. Byeolsu charged up his wristband and touched it to his forehead. Two daggers of light emitted from his hands and threw them at Enceladus' feet. Enceladus backed away.

"Impressive," said Enceladus. "But there is more to this ancient fairytale then meets the eye and ears. I may have a present for you if you do not hurry back to your meek home."

XIII

"These are they who were not defiled with women; they are virgins and these are the ones who follow the Lamb wherever he goes…"

—Revelation 14:4

Zuma was at the ancient hieroglyphs praying in the shadows as a robotic army scoured the forest and trixes ran in front of them right before her eyes. She was certain the time of Charybdis I one was no more. However, she knew that Byeolsu knew of his right to rule Charybdis I since they evacuated to Charybdis II. She knew the planet was not dying despite the insurrection of the miners of the planet and the moons orbiting it, but the insurrection was firmly taking hold. Her daughter Sia was still at the calvet, and so was Errai and Negral.

Zuma gathered herself and summoned a xenozhu to ride to the calvet to inform Errai, Negral, and Sia that they may be taken. If and only if, the calvet is taken by the insurrectionists. Zuma began to pray.

When she reached the calvet, she saw Errai, Negral, and Sia standing outside.

"Where is Byeolsu?" said Negral, his stoicism fading as the impending doom of Charybdis I began to take hold.

"I think he's at the corcova with Cephei," she muttered.

"Well, Zuma, what do you think of your prophesy as the planet's government rips itself apart and insurrectionists are approaching us with its robotic army," said Errai.

"I think I did well," she said. "Our ancestors have proven true about the future of our caste and Byeolsu's well-being."

"And, what about the future of the rest of the Charybdisians and their race and caste? Where will they go?" said Errai furrowing his brow.

"I think Charybdisians would be better on Charybdis II, but not out of concern for their caste and the future of their race," she said as he gave the blessing to Errai.

All three stood in front of the calvet before the hyper center, as it began to shimmer. Sia held hands with Negral. Six robots began to emerge from the hyper center and as son as the materialize. They said, "You are under arrest for being the rulers of Charybdis I as members of the Imperium."

"What is your charge?" said Negral.

"Treason and subjugation of the Charybdis people," said one of the robots.

"I find no grounds for your charge. I was only a councilmember of the Imperial Council, and my family has only done honest work with the Charybdisians remaining who have not been taken by the mining savages on the Council," rebuke Negral.

"That is no excuse," said the robots collectively.

None of the three shivered at the robots' response, and the xenozhu stayed with them as the robots' eyes glowed as the messages from the capital were to eradicate any remaining resistance. The Robots' lifted up their hands and they began to glow. The robots' eyes showed began to wince at the lack of response from the three. But the disconcerting stoicism picked up by the robots was no cause of concern for them. In an instant the robots still murdered the three and the xenozhu and none let out a pathetic scream.

XIV

"Whenever those states which have been acquired as stated have been accustomed to live under their own laws and in freedom, there are three courses for those who wish to hold them: the first to ruin them, the next to reside there in person, the third is to permit them to live under their own laws…"

The Prince, Niccolo Machiavelli

Byeolsu began running through the forest, but in the distance, he saw smoke. Growing more concerned and realizing Enceladus may still be after him, he touched the wrist band and jumped through the hyper center to block any coming attacks from Enceladus. He hit the ground before the hyper center.

Byeolsu found himself on his back and wiped away soil from his eyes. He got up immediately dusting off his clothes and fumbling around with his wrist and head band. Byeolsu let out a scream. He found all three—Sia, Zuma, and Negral—dead, and the calvet burning right before his eyes. He touched his wristband and tried to recalibrate theirs to begin the healing process. The process failed. Byeolsu made his way to the other end of the calvet where his bed was and picked up some orbs hoping that they would offer protection. Byeolsu decided to go to the capital of Orleans to input the code to release himself from the constitution of Charybdis and help him escape to Charybdis II. He saw the insurrectionist spaceships orbiting the planet above him.

Byeolsu grabbed a hover board and zoomed off to Orleans despite hearing marching from a robotic army searching the forest for any survivors. Byeolsu made it to the gate of Orleans and continued to move past the Imperial Towers to the side of the city where the Imperial Council resided. He rushed into the chambers of the Imperial Council. He continued to run to the podium where his father once stood before the insurrection and evacuation. Byeolsu touched his wristband and made sure his recalibration to the constitution on Charybdis II was complete by inserting a specially made prism from the mines only given to the Imperial Council. He also sent an evacuation message to all remaining loyal spaceships to evacuate any remaining Charybdisians. For now, Byeolsu remained safe. He teleported to the neared spaceship and alerted a Captain as to what happened to his family. It was only a matter a chance about the future of Charybdis I and as far Charybdis II he was the future ruler now.

Printed in the United States
By Bookmasters